Wash On!

Michèle Marineau

Illustrations by Manon Gauthier

Translated by Erin Woods

pajamapress

First published in Canada and the United States in 2018

Text copyright © 2018 Michèle Marineau
Illustration copyright © 2018 Manon Gauthier
This edition copyright © 2018 Pajama Press Inc.
Translated from the French by Erin Woods
Originally published by Éditions Québec Amérique inc., 2010

10 9 8 7 6 5 4 3 2 1

www.pajamapress.ca   info@pajamapress.ca

Canada Council   Conseil des arts
for the Arts   du Canada

ONTARIO ARTS COUNCIL
CONSEIL DES ARTS DE L'ONTARIO
an Ontario government agency
un organisme du gouvernement de l'Ontario

Canadä

The publisher gratefully acknowledges the support of the Canada Council for the Arts and the Ontario Arts Council for its publishing program. We acknowledge the financial support of the Government of Canada through the Canada Book Fund (CBF) for our publishing activities.

Library and Archives Canada Cataloguing in Publication

Marineau, Michèle, 1955-
[Barbouillette. English]
      Wash on! / Michèle Marineau ; illustrations by
Manon Gauthier ; translated by Erin Woods.
Translation of: Barbouillette.
ISBN 978-1-77278-018-5 (hardcover)
      I. Gauthier, Manon, 1959-, illustrator   II. Woods, Erin, 1989-, translator
III. Title. IV. Title: Barbouillette. English
PS8576.A657B3713 2018   jC843'.54   C2017-906144-5

Publisher Cataloging-in-Publication Data (U.S.)

Names: Marineau, Michèle, 1955-, author. | Gauthier, Manon, illustrator. | Woods, Erin, translator.
Title: Wash On! / Michèle Marineau ; illustrations by Manon Gauthier ; translated by Erin Woods.
Description: Toronto, Ontario Canada : Pajama Press, 2018. | Previously published in French as "Barbouillette!" | Summary: "When young Petronilla cries "Wash on" instead of "wash off," colors start transferring mysteriously between the little girl and everything she touches. Color chaos spreads around the world, but the delighted Petronilla refuses to undo her mischief. Only the disappearance of her beloved dog convinces her to finally say "Wash off" and return everything to almost normal"— Provided by publisher.
Identifiers: ISBN 978-1-77278-018-5 (hardcover)
Subjects: LCSH: Sisters – Juvenile fiction. | Families – Juvenile fiction. | Humorous stories. | BISAC: JUVENILE FICTION / Imagination & Play.
Classification: LCC PZ7.M375Wa |DDC [E] – dc23

Original art created with mixed media

Manufactured by Friesens
Printed in Canada

Pajama Press Inc.
181 Carlaw Ave. Suite 207 Toronto, Ontario Canada, M4M 2S1

Distributed in Canada by UTP Distribution
5201 Dufferin Street Toronto, Ontario Canada, M3H 5T8

Distributed in the U.S. by Ingram Publisher Services
1 Ingram Blvd. La Vergne, TN 37086, USA

To Catherine when she was five years old, and to Sophie now, with all my love—Michèle

For my friends Azina and Chiwawa—Manon

Mr. and Mrs. Gillis

have two daughters: Babette
and Petronilla.

Babette is perfect.
And Petronilla is…Petronilla.

She has a talent for chaos.

Mrs. Gillis

Mr. Gillis

Babette the Perfect

Petronilla

The dog

One day, Mrs. Gillis tried to give her daughter a bath.

"Wash on!" said Petronilla.
"Not wash on, sweetheart," said her mother. "Wash off. When you wash, the mess comes off. If you washed something *on* it would—"

Petronilla's cheek was blue. Blue like the washcloth.

"Strange," murmured Mrs. Gillis. "Very strange."

She tried a second washcloth. Her daughter's cheek turned green.

A A A A

Babette and her father and the dog all came running. They found the bathroom splattered with splashes of color.

"Wash on!" Petronilla crowed.

Mrs. Gillis furrowed her eyebrows. "Petronilla, say 'Wash off' this instant!"

"Wash on! Wash on! Wash on!" chanted Petronilla.

Oh!

Ah!

Woof!

After that, Petronilla, Babette, and Mr. Gillis touched everything they could find. Each time, the splotches of color transferred from one object to the other. Soon the house looked like a kaleidoscope.

$$D = \frac{1}{c}\frac{1}{\ell}\frac{d\ell}{dt} = \frac{1}{c}\frac{1}{P}\frac{dP}{dt}$$

$$D^2 = \frac{1}{P^2}\frac{P_0 - P}{P} \sim \frac{1}{P^2} \quad (1a)$$

$$D^2 = \frac{K\varrho}{3}\frac{P_0 - P}{P_0} \sim \frac{1}{3}K\varrho \quad (2a)$$

$$D^2 \sim 10^{-53}$$

$$\varrho \sim 10^{-26}$$

$$P \sim 10^8 \, \mathcal{L.J.}$$

$$t \sim 10^{10} (10^{11}) \, \mathcal{J}$$

Mrs. Gillis grumbled, but the others thought it was a delightful day.

The next day was not so much fun.

"I can't go to school like this!" wailed Babette.

"What will happen if I shake somebody's hand?" her father muttered.

Everyone looked at Petronilla.

"Petronilla. Dear Petronilla…please say 'Wash off'!"

Petronilla had never felt so important. She smiled sweetly.

Wash On!

"Don't panic," Mr. Gillis whispered.
"Petronilla will come around soon.
Until then, we'll just stay inside."

But Mr. Gillis was wrong. Petronilla did not come around.

One day passed. Then ten. Then twenty…

The hardest part was thinking up excuses to stay in the house.

By the end of the month, Babette's teacher was threatening to alert the authorities if Babette did not come back to school at once.

"For goodness' sake, Petronilla!" Mrs. Gillis groaned. "Say 'Wash off!' We can't exactly pretend we have the plague."

"Wash on, wash on, wash on!" sang Petronilla.

"Desperate times call for desperate measures," Mrs. Gillis declared. "We're going to see a doctor. There must be some kind of cure for all these colors."

The doctor was flabbergasted by the explosion of colors. He tried to think of a name for the strange condition.

You have all come down with acute Coloritis!

Nothing could stop coloritis.

Coloritis invaded the street, the neighborhood, the town, the country, the continent, and the whole planet. It was more contagious than lice, the chicken pox, OR the plague…but a lot more ridiculous as well.

The problem was that no one could find anything among all those colors.

At the Gillis house, for instance, it was hard to see the difference between the dog or the flower vase or the couch.

Luckily the dog was the only one that barked when it was time for dinner.

But one day, there was no barking. No greetings from a hungry dog. No kisses from a warm and sloppy tongue.

Dog!

"Dog!" Mr. and Mrs. Gillis cried at the tops of their voices.

"Dog!" called Babette in her perfect voice.

"DOG?" screeched Petronilla.

Suddenly, Petronilla went quiet. She thought hard, her forehead creased. Then, in a small voice, she murmured, "Wash off?"

She rubbed a corner of the table with her t-shirt. The colors disappeared!

Petronilla rubbed everything she could find and shouted with all her strength.

Wash Off!

Wash Off!

Wash Off!

After much rubbing and washing, the family found their dog at last. The poor thing had been trapped! Petronilla set him free.

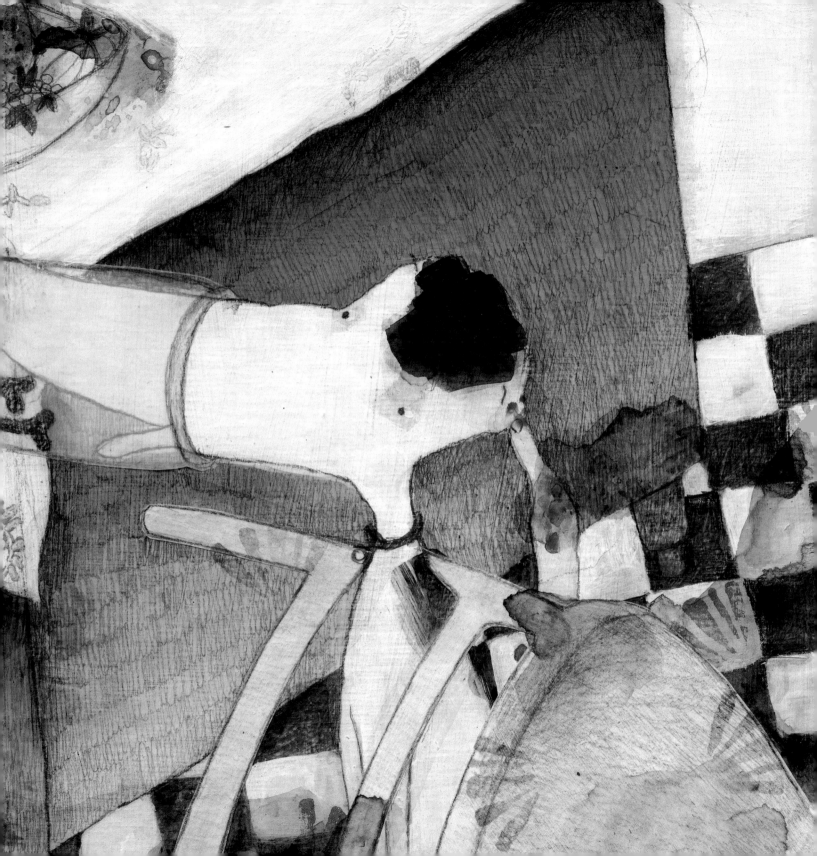

De-coloritis was just as contagious as coloritis.

Soon the house, the street, the neighborhood, the town, the country, the continent, and the entire planet were better than ever.

The whole universe breathed a sigh of relief…
except Petronilla. Sometimes, she found that days
were just a bit too dull.

So, when Petronilla is bored…when Babette is too perfect, or when her mother insists on washing her ears, Petronilla says loudly,

"Wash On!"

just to put a little color into life.

But these outbreaks of coloritis never last long. Petronilla is too afraid to lose her dog again. The dog, by the way, earned a new name after this adventure. He is now called…